Dear Parent:
Your child's love of reading starts here!

Every child learns to read in a different way and at his or her own speed. Some go back and forth between reading levels and read favorite books again and again. Others read through each level in order. You can help your young reader improve and become more confident by encouraging his or her own interests and abilities. From books your child reads with you to the first books he or she reads alone, there are I Can Read Books for every stage of reading:

SHARED READING
Basic language, word repetition, and whimsical illustrations, ideal for sharing with your emergent reader

BEGINNING READING
Short sentences, familiar words, and simple concepts for children eager to read on their own

READING WITH HELP
Engaging stories, longer sentences, and language play for developing readers

READING ALONE
Complex plots, challenging vocabulary, and high-interest topics for the independent reader

ADVANCED READING
Short paragraphs, chapters, and exciting themes for the perfect bridge to chapter books

I Can Read Books have introduced children to the joy of reading since 1957. Featuring award-winning authors and illustrators and a fabulous cast of beloved characters, I standard for beginning readers.

A lifetime of discovery begins with the

D1473825

d!"

Visit www.icanread.com for information
on enriching your child's reading experience.

I Can Read!

BEGINNING
1
READING

Sammy
THE SEAL

story and pictures by **SYD HOFF**

HarperCollins*Publishers*

HarperCollins®, 🐾®, and I Can Read Book® are trademarks of HarperCollins Publishers Inc.

Library of Congress Cataloging-in-Publication Data

Hoff, Syd, date
  Sammy the seal / story and pictures by Syd Hoff.
    p. cm.—(An I can read book)
  Summary: Anxious to see what life is like outside the zoo, Sammy the seal explores the city, goes to school, and plays with the children but decides that there really is no place like home.
    ISBN-10: 0-06-028545-1 (trade bdg.) — ISBN-13: 978-0-06-028545-6 (trade bdg.)
    ISBN-10: 0-06-028546-X (lib. bdg.) — ISBN-13: 978-0-06-028546-3 (lib. bdg.)
    ISBN-10: 0-06-444270-5 (pbk.) — ISBN-13: 978-0-06-444270-1 (pbk.)
    [1. Seals (Animals)—Fiction. 2. Zoos—Fiction. 3. Humorous stories.] I. Title. II. Series.
PZ7.H672Sam 2000
[E]—dc21

99-13805
CIP
AC

❖
12 13 SCP 20 19 18 17 16 15 14 13 12

Sammy
THE SEAL

It was feeding time at the zoo.

All the animals

were getting their food.

The lions ate their meat.

The elephants ate their hay.

The monkeys ate their bananas.

The bears ate their honey.

Then it was time

for the seals to be fed.

Mr. Johnson took them fish.

"Hooray for fish!" said the seals.

They jumped in the water.

Soon the basket was empty.

"That is all there is," said Mr. Johnson.

"There is no more."

"Thank you for the fish," said the seals.

"They were good."

The seals were happy.

But one little seal was not happy.

He sat by himself.

He looked sad.

"What is wrong, Sammy?"

said Mr. Johnson.

"I want to know

what it is like

outside the zoo," said the little seal.

"I want to go out and look around."

"All right, Sammy," said Mr. Johnson.

"You have been a good seal.

You may go out and see."

"Good-bye, Sammy," said the other seals.

"Have a good time."

"Good-bye," said Sammy.

"Where are you going?" said the zebra.

"I am going out," said Sammy.

"Have fun," said the hippo.

"Come back soon," said the giraffe.

Sammy walked and walked and walked.

He did not know what to look at first.

"That seal must be from out of town,"
said a man.

Sammy looked at everything.

"What street is this?" said a man.

"I am a stranger here myself,"
said Sammy.

"I guess it is feeding time here, too,"
said Sammy.

"That is a lovely fur coat," said a lady.

"Where did you get it?"

"I was born with it," said Sammy.

"I wish I could find some water.
I am hot. I want to go swimming,"
said Sammy.

"We are sorry. There is no room for you in this puddle," said the birds.

"And there is no room for you here,"
said the goldfish.

"Keep out," said the policeman.

"You cannot swim in there."

"Ah, here is a place!" said Sammy.

"Who is in my bathtub?" said someone.

"I am sorry," said Sammy.

He left at once.

Some children were standing in line.

Sammy got in line, too.

"What are we waiting for?"

asked Sammy.

"School. What do you think?" said a boy.

"That will be fun.

I will come, too," Sammy said.

The teacher was not looking.

Sammy sat down.

The children made words with blocks.

Sammy wished he could spell.

"All right, children.

Now we will all sing a song,"

said the teacher.

The children had good voices.

"That sounds fine," said the teacher.

"But one of you is barking—

just like a seal."

"Is it you, Joey?"

said the teacher.

"No," said Joey.

"Is it you, Helen?"
said the teacher.
"No," said Helen.

"Is it you, Dorothy, Robert, Fred, Joan, or Agnes?"

"No," said the children.

"Then it must be you,"

said the teacher.

"I am sorry. This school is just for boys and girls."

"Please let me stay," said Sammy.

"I will be good."

"All right. You may stay,"

said the teacher.

Sammy was happy.

He sat at his desk

and looked at the teacher.

He learned how to read.

He learned how to write.

"And now it is time to play,"

said the teacher.

"Who wants to play a game?"

"We do," said the children.

They threw the ball over the net.

"The ball must not hit the ground,"
cried Sammy's team.

"Somebody catch the ball."

Sammy caught the ball on his nose!

A boy on the other team tried
to catch the ball on his nose, too.
"Boys must catch with their hands,"
said the teacher.

Sammy tried to catch the ball
with his flippers.

"Seals must catch with their noses,"
said the teacher.

Up and down went the ball,

from one side to the other.

At last the teacher blew her whistle.

"Who wins?" said the children.

"It is even," said the teacher.

Everybody was happy.

A bell rang. School was over.

"Will you be here tomorrow?"

said the children.

"No," said Sammy.

"School is fun,

but I belong in the zoo.

I just wanted to know

what it is like outside.

Now I have to go back."

"Good-bye, Sammy," said the children.

"We will come to see you."

"Good," said Sammy.

Sammy was in a hurry

to get back to the zoo.

He had so much to tell the other seals.

"May I welcome you home, Sammy,"

said Mr. Johnson.

"I am glad you are back.

You are just in time for dinner."

"There's no place like home,"
said Sammy.